For Aunt Barbara, who never gave up on her dreams... or mine.

With love and gratitude to Liz and Nikki for sharing this journey with me.

Text copyright © 2014 by Alyson H. Flippo
Illustrations copyright © 2014 by Kathleen Murphy Willer

All rights reserved, including the right to reproduce in whole or in part in any form.

Printed in China

Addie B. Strong

Dream Big

Alyson Flippo & Kathleen Murphy Willer

It was a day to remember,

That day in September,

When Addie B. got her chance

To get up and dance.

It began one day
   As she lay in her bed,

   Petting her cat
      And resting her head.

"I want to dance," she thought to herself.

Just like the ballerina that sat on her shelf.

The dance troupe at school was doing a show.
She wanted to join, to learn and to grow.

So she practiced for hours, for days and for weeks.
She practiced till the color rose high in her cheeks.

When she was invited
  To dance on the team,

She was over the moon;
  She had found her dream.

That was until
   She overheard

The other girls utter
   Some very mean words:

"Addie B. Strong," they said from afar,

"Is not quite as good as the rest of us are."

"Perhaps they are right," She said to herself.

"I don't look much Like the ballerina on my shelf."

Addie's legs were quite short
And her arms very long,

And she began to doubt
If she really was strong.

The day finally came,
 The show would soon start,

But she was still a bit nervous
 As she walked through the park.

Just then she happened
Upon Collin B. Kind,

Sitting on a bench,
Enjoying the sunshine.

"Hello, Cousin Collin,
So glad to see you!"

And she sat down beside him
To lace up her shoes.

"I'm on my way to my show,
But I'm scared and afraid.

The other girls have beautiful hair
In ponytails and braids."

As Collin helped Addie
Tie up her knot,

He smiled and reminded her
Of that which she forgot.

"Oh Addie," he said.
"You're special cause you're you!"

And as she thought about these words,
she remembered they were true.

With that she stood taller
And bravely shouted "Yes!"

"You are right," she declared.
"I just need to do my best."

As Addie set off,
   She kept Collin's words in mind.

The strength that she needed
   Was in her own heart to find.

On that lovely September day,
Addie danced her fears away.

For Addie again found what she knew all along,
She was amazing and unique,
She was beautiful and STRONG.

And just as Addie

Dreamed from her heart,

DREAM BIG and reach for the stars.

The only thing you need to do
Is just love who you are.

THE END

(For now. . .)